worried worried worried worried worried worried worried worried worried worried worried worried worried worried

worried worried worried worried worried worried worried worried worried

worried worried worried worried worried worried worried worr

rried worried worried worried worried worried

ed worried worried worried worried

Worried Worried Worrie

IED WORRIED WORRI

ORRIED

RIED

SIMON & SCHUSTER BOOKS FOR YOUNG READERS • An imprint of Simon & Schuster Children's Publishing Division • 1230 Avenue of the Americas, New York, New York 10020 • Text © 2019 by Hot Schwartz Productions • Illustration © 2019 by Debbie Ridpath Ohi • Book design by Laurent Linn © 2019 by Simon & Schuster, Inc. •

Cafeteria. • The illustrations for this book were rendered digitally. • Manufactured in China • 0521 SCP • First Simon & Schuster Books for Young Readers paperback edition August 2021 • 10 9 8 7 6 5 4 3 2 1 • The hardcover edition August 2021 • 10 9 8 7 6 5 Library of Congress has cataloged the hardcover edition as follows: Names: Black, Michael Ian, Ridpath, 1962– 1971– author. | Ohi, Debbie / Michael Ian illustrator. | Title: I'm worried Ridpath Ohi. Black ; illustrated by Debbie Description: First • Other titles: I am worried Schuster Books for edition. | New York : Simon & Potato is worried about what might happen in the future, causing Flamingo to worry, too, but their friend, a little girl, encourages them to focus on enjoying the present, instead. • Identifiers: LCCN 2018013151 (print) | LCCN 2018019265 (ebook) | ISBN 9781534415867 (hardcover : alk. paper) | ISBN 9781665904988 (pbk) | ISBN 9781534415874 (eBook) • Subjects: | CYAC: Worry—Fiction. | Best friends— Fiction. | Friendship—Fiction. | Potatoes—Fiction. | Flamingos— Fiction. • Classification: LCC PZ7.B5292 (ebook) | LCC PZ7.B5292 It 2019 (print) | DDC [E]—dc23 • LC record available at https://lccn.loc.gov/2018013151

For the worriers. Take a breath.
Right now, in this moment, you are fine.
And this moment is all that matters.
—M. I. B.

For my dear friend Beckett, who told me
not to worry—it made all the difference
—D. R. O.

I'M WORRIED

By Michael Ian Black

Illustrated by Debbie Ridpath Ohi

SIMON & SCHUSTER BOOKS FOR YOUNG READERS
New York   London   Toronto   Sydney   New Delhi

I'm worried.

What are you worried about?

The future.

Why are you worried about the future?

Because what if something **BAD** happens?

Please tell me nothing bad will ever happen.

I wish I could, Potato, but I can't.

Because **nobody** knows what's going to happen.

WHY NOT???

Um, now I'M worried.

It's okay, you two. Sometimes bad things happen.

Like, Potato, remember that time you rolled off the table?

I was bruised for **weeks**.

And, Flamingo, remember when

you got your beak stuck in the peanut butter jar?

Peanut butter is the worst.

And that time I fell off the monkey bars and broke my arm?

All of those things were bad at first . . .

I got a sticker at the doctor's office and it was **scratch 'n' sniff!**

Power to the Potato

I put bologna on my sandwich and it was **delicious!**

You both doodled all over my cast
and it looked awesome!

I'm going to wrap
myself in
Bubble Wrap,
just in case.

That way nothing bad
can happen again!

Guys . . .

Guys . . .

guys?

It's getting very
warm in here.

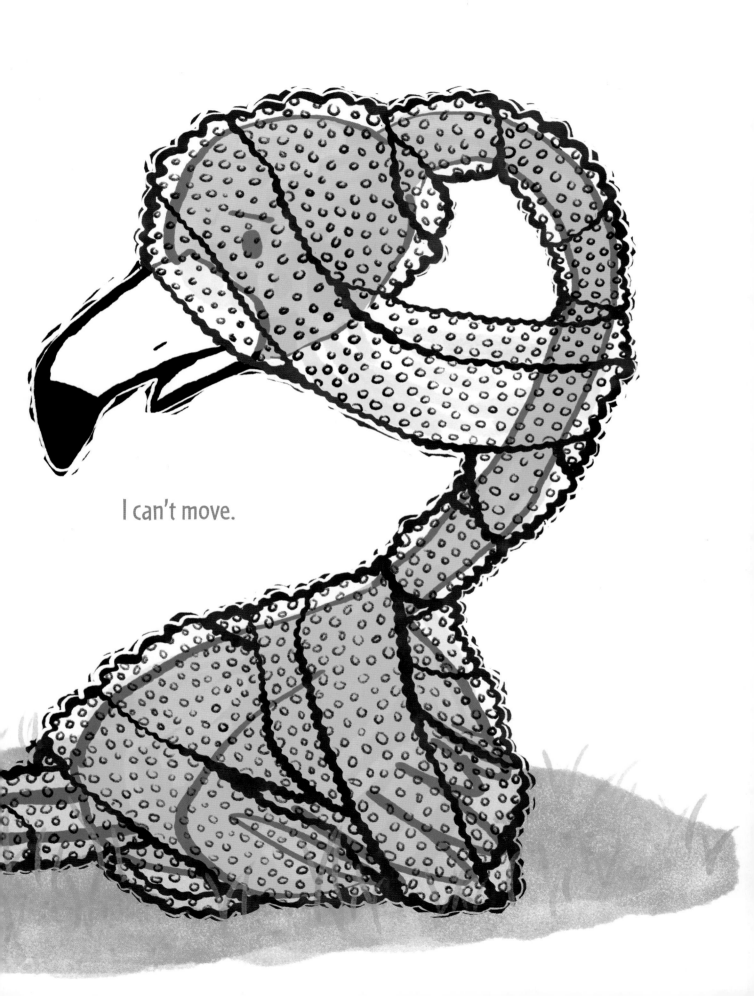

I can't move.

See?

Worrying doesn't help!

Since we **don't** know what's going to happen in the future, maybe we should just **enjoy** the **now**.

Enjoy the **now**?

Am I doing it right?

Yup.

How about **NOW**?

You got it!

Hey, Flamingo.

Yeah?

Enjoying the now is **way** better than worrying about the future!

(But peanut butter
is still the worst.)

worried worried worried worried worried worried worried worried worried worried worried worried worried

worried worried worried worried worried worried worried worried worried worried worried

worried worried worried worried worried worried worried

worried worried worried worried worried worried

worried worried worried worried w

Worried Worried Worrie

ORRIED WORRIED WO

WORRIED W

WORRIE

WOR

worried worried worried worried worried worried worried worried worried worried worried worried worried worried

orried worried worried worried worried worried worried worried worried worried

worried worried worried worried worried worried worried worried

rried worried worried worried worried worried worried

d worried worried worried worried

Worried Worried Worrie

IED WORRIED WORRI

ORRIED

RIED